The Little, Little House

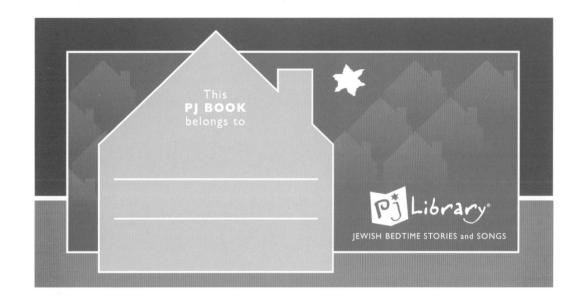

This
PJ BOOK
belongs to

_____

_____

PJ Library®

JEWISH BEDTIME STORIES and SONGS

About the story

This is a Jewish folktale from Eastern Europe. In most versions it is the village rabbi
who puts things right, or sometimes a wise neighbour. I have based my heroine, Aunty Bella,
on my mother's great-aunt. She came from the Ukraine where she was the wise woman of the village.
As in the story, everyone took their troubles to her and she always had an answer.

The Little, Little House copyright © Frances Lincoln Limited 2005
Text, illustrations and design copyright © Jessica Souhami and Paul McAlinden 2005

First published in Great Britain and the USA in 2005 by
Frances Lincoln Children's Books, 74-77 White Lion Street, London N1 9PF
www.franceslincoln.com

Distributed in the USA by Publishers Group West

First paperback edition published in Great Britain in 2006 and in the USA in 2007

British Library Cataloguing in Publication Data
available on request

051521.5K1/B0634
ISBN 10: 1-84507-283-9
ISBN 13: 978-1-84507-283-4

The illustrations are collage and crayon
Set in Gill Sans and Sabon

Printed in China

9 8 7 6 5 4 3 2 1

JESSICA SOUHAMI studied at the Central School of Art and Design. In 1980 she formed Mme Souhami and Co., a travelling puppet company using colourful shadow puppets with a musical accompaniment and a storyteller. Her books for Frances Lincoln are just as vibrant and funny as her puppet shows. They include *The Leopard's Drum*, *Rama and the Demon King*, *No Dinner!*, *In the Dark, Dark Wood*, *Mrs McCool and the Giant Cúchulainn*, *The Famous Adventure of a Bird-Brained Hen* and *Sausages*. She lives in North London.

The Little, Little House

Jessica Souhami

F

FRANCES LINCOLN
CHILDREN'S BOOKS

Long ago, before you were even born,
there was a poor man called Joseph
who lived in a little, little house with his wife
and three children.

There was a yard in the front
with six yellow chickens
and a red rooster pecking the dirt.

And there was a field at the back
with a pretty brown cow
and a little grey goat chewing the grass.

And Joseph knew they could never be happy
in such a little, little house.

"How can we be happy?" Joseph sighed.
"We're so jammed and crammed, so squashed and squeezed.
There's no money for a bigger house. So what can I do?"

Suddenly he thought, "I know! I'll ask Aunty Bella."

Aunty Bella was clever and kind.
She listened to everyone's problems
and always gave good advice.

So the next day Joseph went to see Aunty Bella.

"Aunty Bella," he said,
"we can never be happy
in such a little, little house.
What can I do?"

Aunty Bella just smiled.

"Go home, Joseph," she said,

"and take the six yellow chickens
into your house.

See what a difference
that will make!"

And Joseph did as Aunty Bella said.

But THIS is what happened ...

So the next day Joseph went back to see Aunty Bella.

"Aunty Bella," he said, "things are worse!

Our house is so full, it's creaking!

And the chickens are SO CHEEKY!

What can I do?"

Aunty Bella just smiled.

"Go home, Joseph," she said,

"and take the red rooster
into the house.

See what a difference
that will make!"

And Joseph did as Aunty Bella said.

But THIS is what happened ...

So the next day Joseph went back to see Aunty Bella.

"Aunty Bella," he said, "things are dreadful!

Our house is so full, it's shaking!

The chickens are so cheeky.

And the rooster's SO NOISY!
What can I do?"

Aunty Bella just smiled.

"Go home, Joseph," she said,

"and take the pretty brown
cow into the house.

See what a difference
that will make!"

And Joseph did as Aunty Bella said.

But THIS is what happened ...

So the next day Joseph went back to see Aunty Bella.

"Aunty Bella," he said, "things are terrible!

Our house is so full, it's quaking!

The chickens are so cheeky.

The rooster's so noisy.

And the cow's SO CLUMSY!

What can I do?"

Aunty Bella just smiled.

"Go home, Joseph," she said,

"and take the little grey goat into the house.

See what a difference that will make!"

And Joseph did as Aunty Bella said.

But THIS is what happened ...

So the next day Joseph went back to see Aunty Bella.

"Aunty Bella," he said, "things are impossible!
Our house is so full, it's bursting!
The chickens are so cheeky.
The rooster's so noisy.
The cow's so clumsy.
And the goat's SO SMELLY!
What can I do?"

Aunty Bella laughed out loud.

"Go home, Joseph," she said,

"and turn all the animals
out of the house.

See what a difference
that will make!"

And Joseph did as Aunty Bella said.

And THIS is what happened ...

"How peaceful it is," sighed Joseph.
"How quiet and clean.
Our house is not so little, little after all."
He smiled, "How happy we are."

And the next day ...

... Joseph went to thank clever Aunty Bella.

MORE TITLES BY JESSICA SOUHAMI
FROM FRANCES LINCOLN CHILDREN'S BOOKS

The Famous Adventure of a Bird-Brained Hen

Henny Penny was so bird-brained that when an acorn fell, BOP! on her head,
she thought the sky must be falling. She set out at once to tell the king,
collecting her silly friends along the way. But Foxy Loxy was always just ahead
and he was HUNGRY. So did Henny Penny get to see the king?
And did Foxy Loxy eat a good dinner that night?

ISBN 0-7112-2026-3 (UK)
ISBN 1-84507-263-4 (US)

The Leopard's Drum

Osebo the leopard has a fine, a huge, a magnificent drum,
but he won't let anyone else have it – not even Nyame the Sky-god.
So Nyame offers a big reward to the animal who will bring him the drum...
How a very small tortoise outwits the boastful leopard is retold
by Jessica Souhami in this traditional tale from West Africa.

ISBN 0-7112-0907-3 (UK)
ISBN 1-84507-506-4 (US)

Rama and the Demon King

This story from the Ramayana tells of the brave and good prince Rama
and his battle against Ravana, the evil ten-headed king of all the demons.

ISBN 0-7112-1158-2 (UK)
ISBN 1-84507-361-4 (US)

Frances Lincoln titles are available from all good bookshops.
You can also buy books and find out more about your favourite titles,
authors and illustrators on our website: www.franceslincoln.com